Not-So-Normal Norman

Text copyright © 1995 by Cynthia Stowe.
Illustrations copyright © 1995 by Cat Bowman Smith.
Published in 1995 by Albert Whitman & Company,
6340 Oakton Street, Morton Grove, Illinois 60053-2723.
Published simultaneously in Canada by General Publishing, Limited,
Toronto. All rights reserved. No part of this book may be reproduced or
transmitted in any form or by any means, electronic or mechanical,
including photocopying, recording, or by any information storage and
retrieval system, without permission in writing from the publisher.
Printed in the United States of America.
10 9 8 7 6 5 4 3 2 1

The text is set in Trump Mediaeval.
The illustration medium is pen and ink.
Design by Karen A. Yops

Library of Congress Cataloging-in-Publication Data

Stowe, Cynthia.
Not-so-normal Norman / Cynthia Stowe ;
illustrated by Cat Bowman Smith.
p. cm.
Summary: While his father is out of work because of a
back injury, Anthony decides to try to earn money, and
his first job is watching a huge tarantula named Norman.
ISBN 0-8075-5767-6
[1. Moneymaking projects—Fiction. 2. Tarantulas—
Fiction. 3. Family life—Fiction.] I. Smith, Cat Bowman, ill.
II. Title.
PZ7.S8915No 1995
[Fic]—dc20   94-255
                                                                          CIP
                                                                          AC

To Robert,
who is helping me learn to love
all my "tarantulas."

CS

Thanks to Amy Parrill for letting me help her pet-sit the beagle, which led to the original concept for this story. Thanks to Tina Lankowski for the name "A Cut Above," Nat Waring for information about carpentry, and to Dr. Jamie Elkin and Dr. Virginia Elkin for information on chiropractic.

Many thanks to Kerry Taylor, who runs Creature Comforts, an excellent pet-sitting business, and to Kerry's cats, Peaches and Sunny Jim, who inspire her. Thanks, also, to Susan English.

As always, great appreciation goes to members of my critique group: Michael Daley, Jessie Haas, Winifred Luhrmann, Lorraine Ryan, Jean Shaw, and especially to Nancy Wilson, who read the manuscript "one last time."

Thank you to Karen Burand, D.V.M., for checking the story. Thanks to Liza Voges, my agent, and to Kathleen Tucker and Judith Mathews at Albert Whitman and Company.

Not-So-Normal Norman
by Cynthia Stowe

illustrated by Cat Bowman Smith

Albert Whitman & Company, Morton Grove, Illinois

1

Crash! The noise behind him made Anthony jump. He grabbed James's arm for balance.

"Look out!" James said. "You almost made me drop *my* tray."

"Sorry."

The other kids were standing around watching Lisa's milk drift farther into her spilled spaghetti. There she was on the floor next to her lunch. Anthony bent down to help her, but then saw Mr. Valeski coming toward them.

Anthony stood up quickly and grabbed James's arm a second time. "Let's go."

"What?"

"Let's go!" Anthony walked quickly to the farthest corner of the fourth grade section of the cafeteria.

James followed. "How come you didn't get a tray?" he asked. "You love eating spaghetti."

"Sit down. I don't want Mr. Valeski to see me. He'll ask why I'm not having lunch."

"You sick?" James asked. "You don't look sick." James plopped his solid body down beside his friend.

Anthony pushed his glasses higher up on his nose. He watched Mr. Valeski sponging the floor.

Anthony hated to admit it, but even with the milk mixing into it, Lisa's spaghetti had looked good. He sighed.

It was going to be a long and hungry afternoon.

"Didn't your mom give you a dollar?" James grabbed his fork. "She always gives you money on spaghetti day. Besides, if she hadn't given you a dollar, she'd have given you a bag lunch."

Anthony looked away, hoping that James's conversation with himself would quickly end.

"Just tell me and get it over with," James said.

Anthony wished he could slide under the table. But James was right; he might as well get it over with. "I'm gonna give the money back to Mom."

James didn't laugh. They'd been friends

a long time, since kindergarten. James knew that Anthony must have a good reason.

James finally sighed. "You gotta eat *something*," he said. He handed Anthony his brownie.

"I'm not gonna eat your lunch."

"Take it, or I'll tell."

Anthony knew that James would never tell, not for anything, but he took the brownie gratefully and ate it slowly, flicking each crumb around his mouth.

Anthony's parents needed the money ever since his dad had hurt his back and couldn't work as a carpenter anymore. Mom was still working her full-time job as a salesperson in the fabric department at Fenton's. But now she was taking in mending, too.

Anthony's extra dollar might help to

take away the worried look on Mom's face.

James interrupted his thoughts. "What are you gonna tell her about how you got the money?"

"I'm gonna tell her I found it."

"She might believe it once, but not more than that."

James was right. Anthony was going to have to think of something better for future spaghetti days.

"Well, maybe you could tell her you won a prize at school." James shook his head. "No, she wouldn't believe that. They only give us pencils or a book, even if it's a big deal."

"James."

"What?"

"Be quiet—I have to think." Anthony took his glasses off and sat fiddling with them. Finally, he turned his chair to look around. The cafeteria was emptying.

Katie D. and Jonathan, the sixth graders who had cafeteria duty, were already carrying the milk carton recycling bins into the kitchen. They were working hard. They were—

"I got it!" Anthony said. "I'll tell her I earned the money." Anthony rolled up the sleeves of his denim jacket. "Hey, James, maybe I *could* earn it. Maybe I could get a job and make some money."

"Doing what? I mean, you could clean stuff, but you hate doing that and—"

"I'll think of something. I will."

Anthony turned back to the table. "You gonna finish that spaghetti?"

James passed the tray over. "Eat it. Then I'll go try to get seconds."

2

"You sure have a good appetite tonight, Anthony." Dad was sounding better. He was actually at the table, not eating exactly, but sitting with them and having a cup of coffee. His long body was less scrunched over.

Anthony nodded and plunked another piece of meatloaf in his mouth. He reached down to Speckles McGraw, who was rubbing against his legs. Anthony patted her soft black head.

"Don't pick up that cat at the table," Mom said, even though she knew Anthony wouldn't. Mom had been repeating the rules a lot lately.

She'd started doing it this past summer when Dad got fewer calls for work. Decks and porches, stairs and landings: that was what Dad built. He had his own one-man business: A Cut Above Carpentry.

Dad got such little work this past summer that he had dropped the insurance that would give him money if he got sick or hurt. So one day when he stepped backwards off a porch and fell and hurt his back, he lost all his income.

"Stay in bed and rest," the doctor had told him.

Dad *had* rested, for weeks now. But he still wasn't getting any better.

These past weeks, since Dad had become bent over, so had Mom, just a little. She didn't bounce around the house anymore.

"Are you feeling better, Leonard?" Mom asked.

Anthony chewed harder on his carrot stick. Why did she have to keep asking Dad that? He never answered, only grunted and looked away.

"I tried that new doctor this morning," Dad said.

Both Anthony and Mom stopped chewing. Wow, Dad was talking about it, talking to both of them, at the dinner table. He was talking to them about his visit to the new doctor, the chiropractor.

"She took X-rays. She doesn't think the disks are ruptured. She thinks she can help me without any surgery."

Mom dropped her fork and covered her mouth with her hands. What was wrong? Wasn't that good news? Dad didn't seem unhappy. Anthony ran to him, and Dad drew him close.

Mom was crying and smiling at the same time. Oh, *that* was it. She was relieved.

"This is gonna work, I can feel it. This doctor's gonna help me. I'm going to be okay." Dad was still talking. After weeks of not talking, not talking to Anthony who he'd always talked to before, talked and laughed and joked and played catch with in the small backyard of their apartment, Dad was talking again!

"She thinks it'll take a month or so, but she says I should start feeling better soon. I still won't be able to work for a while—she was guessing six weeks—and the visits are expensive. It costs—"

"That doesn't matter," Mom said. She almost sounded mad. "The only important thing is that you're going to be okay." She got up and leaned over and kissed Dad and then wiped her eyes. "Now if you're going to get better, you've got to start eating." Without asking, she walked over to the counter and grabbed a plate from the cupboard. She put some mashed potatoes on it and some corn and a piece of the meatloaf, and then heated it in the microwave.

"Pretty soon you're going to make me eat my spinach," Dad said as he released Anthony from his grasp and turned to the table. But Dad was smiling, and he ate everything on his plate.

✳✳✳

Before he went to sleep, Anthony made a list. If Dad couldn't work for six weeks, Anthony still needed to get a job. Under the covers, using his flashlight, he wrote:

sell stuff

clean stuff

wash cars

be a paperboy

This was hard. The words looked okay on the paper, but Anthony couldn't really see himself doing any of it. Maybe the paperboy, but—

Speckles jumped on the bed and pushed her face against Anthony's hand.

"Hey, go away, I'm thinking," Anthony said, rubbing her ears a little so her feelings wouldn't get hurt.

Speckles licked his finger then and sat upright, watching Anthony. She meowed.

"What's your problem? I'm thinking—
I've got work to do. I've got to . . ."

Speckles meowed again, and Anthony
looked at her longer then, a thought
entering. Of course—it was the perfect job!
Anthony loved animals, and he was good
with them. He'd had an ant colony in
kindergarten. And last year in third grade,
he'd taken home Petrovska, the white
mouse, for Christmas vacation, and played
with him every day and cleaned his cage.
He'd been especially careful to keep
Speckles away so that Petrovska wouldn't
get nervous.

Speckles meowed again, loudly this
time, as though she, too, was remembering
Petrovska. Anthony threw off the covers
and picked her up and held her on his
shoulder.

It was the perfect solution. He couldn't

wait to tell James. James would help him make the posters. He was good at that. The posters would go something like:

Are you going on vacation? Do you need someone to pet-sit your dog or cat or whatever?

Anthony liked that last part. Maybe he'd get some interesting animal like a rat. *No animal refused,* he would add.

But there would be too many words for a poster. It'd be too hard to make them look neat and eye-catching. Anthony picked up his paper and pencil and wrote:

I'll take care of your animal.

See Anthony

435 Cherry St.
Third Floor

3

They got the posters done the next afternoon, using the felt pen set James had gotten for his birthday. They decided on:

Pets
I like them.
I'll take care of them.
See Anthony
435 Cherry St., third floor
257-6642
P.S. No pets refused.

"You sure we should've put that last part in?" James asked. "Somebody might have an elephant or a—"

"Who's going to have an elephant around here? Gimme the tacks." Anthony was hanging up the first poster at the laundromat down at the corner of Athens and Elm.

Mrs. Roselle, a neighbor from across the street, pushed the door open with her laundry basket and came down the aisle. She placed her basket on the floor two washers down and bent down and opened a bottle. A strong smell of bleach entered the room.

"Oh, my," she said, noticing the poster. "Anthony, does your mother know you're doing this? Seems to me you're a little young. I don't know if I'd trust someone your age. But, of course. . ." She was stuffing her clothes in the washer now, adding the soap and the bleach.

At least now she'll close the bottle, Anthony thought. He wished that she'd shut something else, too, but Mrs. Roselle had already made him worry. What if Mom didn't let him do it? What if everybody thought he was too young?

What if—Anthony stopped. He wouldn't let himself "what if" anymore. It reminded him that Dad and he used to play "what if" for fun, on rainy afternoons. Before Dad was sick, of course.

"What if I were a monster with a mouth like a pitchfork?" Anthony would say.

"Then I'd throw a pile of dirt in your mouth and give you something to chew on."

They'd both be laughing by then.

Anthony put another tack in the bottom of the poster, pressing it hard into the corkboard. "C'mon, James," he said. "We gotta finish putting these up." He held out the other five posters.

He wasn't going to let Mrs. Roselle stop him. Dad and Mom needed the money. Just this morning, Dad had gotten mad at Mom because she hadn't bought her special tea again.

"It's a luxury," she'd said. "I can do without."

"You love that tea," Dad had answered. "I'm just going to go out and get it myself."

"You can't, Leonard. You're only supposed to walk that much when you go to the chiropractor's!"

"If you don't get it tonight, I will—I promise. I won't have you giving up—"

"All right, you win."

It had sounded like they were mad at each other. But Mom had gone over and kissed Dad on the forehead before she'd gone to work, and she'd kissed Anthony, too, pulling him close.

Mom needed money for her tea, and Anthony was going to earn it. Anthony put a third tack into his poster on the laundromat community board and turned to face Mrs. Roselle.

"Goodbye, Mrs. Roselle." Then he added, not wanting to be rude, "I hope your wash turns out good."

Nothing happened until four-thirty that afternoon. James and Anthony played Connect Four and Crazy Eights while they waited for a customer, whispering in Anthony's bedroom so that Dad could sleep. They waited forever, it seemed, for the doorbell or the phone to ring. Instead, there was a knock on the door.

"Who is it?" Anthony asked.

"I've come about the pet-sitting," a voice answered.

Anthony turned the latch and opened the door.

"Well, you must be the enterprising young man I read about," an old lady said.

She's probably going to tell me I shouldn't do it, Anthony thought, remembering Mrs. Roselle.

The lady didn't seem to notice he wasn't answering. "Well, well, you look just like the type of person who'd make such a fine poster," she said. "And who is your young friend?"

"Oh, uh, this is James," Anthony said. "Would you care to come in?"

"Don't mind if I do. Now, yes, thank you, the chair is lovely."

Anthony got a chance to look at her then. She was a small woman, but not bent over like some older people he'd seen. Her hair was all wild and frizzy, like she'd had a perm that'd gone bad. She'd pinned a purple ribbon on the side and a yellow one in back. It seemed that her hair was exactly the way she liked it.

"Well, well, you're the answer to my prayers,"she said, "absolutely the answer to my prayers. I haven't known *what* to do about him, and he gets so *lonely* when I'm away, and there's so much prejudice, you wouldn't believe how much prejudice we're up against."

Anthony cleared his throat and pushed

his glasses back up on his nose. James coughed.

"So, you can imagine my relief when I saw your fine poster and learned that, of all things, here you are right on my street!"

"You live here?" Anthony asked.

"Two houses down, the yellow and brown. Second floor. Just moved in last Saturday. Well, well, I won't take up anymore of your valuable time. Now, I'll have to get your references, of course."

"But I don't have any—I'm just a kid."

"Of course you have references. You're a person, aren't you?"

"I suppose you can talk to my mom and dad."

"See? Perfect. Now, I'll have to introduce you to Norman—"

"Who is Norman? Is Norman your

husband?" Anthony asked.

"Oh, no, dear," she laughed. "I'm not married. I've never found anybody even remotely interesting enough to marry. My work—I'm a biologist—has always kept me company. Now, how does two dollars a day sound to you?"

Wow, two dollars! Two dollars a day! Anthony was so excited he could only nod.

"And of course, I'll have to give you a list of instructions." She stood up and shook Anthony's hand. "I can't tell you what a relief this is. Those airline people are so . . . so silly about Norman, after that one little time that he got away from me, just when I was letting him have a little exercise on my dinner tray. They say that *women* scream. Well—can you imagine it?—that man next to me was shrieking, and the man in back kept trying to hit

Norman with his umbrella! I was fright-
ened, I'll tell you!"

Anthony nodded sympathetically. Who
was Norman?

"And those pet-sitting people, those . . .
those . . . those . . . grown-ups! They
wouldn't even talk to me about taking care
of him. Just because he's not so . . . not so
normal."

"Miss . . . Miss . . ."

"Yes, dear?"

"Who is Norman?"

"Oh, how silly of me. You mean I
haven't told you? Oh, my. Norman, my
dear, is my tarantula." She got up and
headed for the door. "Now, my flight is at
nine, so I'll be over around six to meet
your parents and leave off Norman."

She shook Anthony's hand and James's,
too, and then headed to the door. She

slammed it behind her.

James turned to Anthony, wide-eyed. "Who is she?" he asked, for once not answering his own question.

"Uh-oh." Anthony sat down, almost missing the chair behind him. "Uh-oh." He realized that she'd never told them her name.

4

Anthony tried to tell them about
Norman at supper, but there were other
things to think about. Dad was eating
meals with them again, and it was so nice
to have him there, even though he was
looking as if his back was hurting.

"Are you all right?" Mom asked.

"The doctor says it's going to take
some time," Dad answered. "It's just that
it's late, and I'm tired."

Dad must be really sick! He'd spent the whole afternoon in bed, and he was still tired? Anthony stabbed a potato, but then he squished it around his plate, not feeling hungry anymore.

"Don't play with your food," Mom said.

Anthony took a small bite, but it tasted funny.

"What's that?" Dad asked. "It sounds like someone's at the door."

Uh-oh, he hadn't told them yet! "I'll get it." Anthony jumped up, hoping it wasn't Miss . . . Miss Whatever Her Name Was.

But his prayers were not answered. Standing in the doorway, a five-gallon fish tank in hand, was Miss Whatever. She'd changed the purple hair ribbon to a green one and was dressed for traveling. She

wore a long blue trench coat that reached almost to the floor, and she carried a large bag over her shoulder.

"Ah, my fine young tarantula-sitter," she said, moving past Anthony into the kitchen. "And you must be this young entrepreneur's parents." She placed the fish tank on the table next to the green beans.

Anthony came close. There in the fish tank was the biggest spider he had ever seen. It was as big as his hand! It had a shiny black body with orange-red spots on its legs. Tan rings bordered the spots. Anthony thought it . . . he . . . Norman . . . was beautiful. But still, Anthony was glad that the fish tank was covered by a strong wire mesh.

"He's a Mexican red-leg," Miss Whatever said.

Mom bent closer to examine the fish tank. She gasped. Dad started to get up, then sat back down again.

"No, no, no," Miss Whatever said. "Now, there's no reason to be afraid. People keep bees, don't they? Most tarantula bites are like bee stings. And Norman is a perfectly civilized tarantula, more civilized, I'll tell you, than that collie next door."

Mom nodded weakly. The collie always barked at Mom when she came home from work.

Speckles came over and rubbed against Mom's legs.

"And who is this lovely creature?" Miss Whatever asked, bending down to stroke the cat. "Pretty, very pretty." But she didn't wait for an answer. "Now, Anthony," Miss Whatever continued,

"I'll be gone for two weeks."

She pulled a plastic container out of her shoulder bag. The container had holes pierced in the top. Miss Whatever opened the lid and put in a piece of lettuce she'd gotten from somewhere else in her bag. The container was filled with live insects.

"Crickets," Miss Whatever said. "Norman loves them. Now, I fed him just before I came over, so you don't need to feed him for a couple of days. Lots of tarantulas only eat once a week, but Norman likes to eat one or two crickets every other day. One thing I can always depend on is my Norman's appetite! And *I* wouldn't want to wait a week for my meal, would *you*?" She chuckled.

Anthony thought that the *crickets* might want him to wait. He wasn't going to like this part.

42

"Can I pick him up?" he asked.

"I don't advise it," Miss Whatever said. "Norman's very sensitive, doesn't like to be handled too much, and he *can* bite if he gets upset. You allergic to anything?"

"No."

"Still, better not to chance it. You have to be careful with all creatures. And you wouldn't know if you were allergic until you were bitten. When I get back, I'll show you how to handle him. He'll be used to you by then. Oh, and here's your list of instructions. I can see that I'm leaving Norman with a very responsible person."

She reached over and grabbed Mom's hand. Mom's arm shook like wet laundry in the wind as Miss Whatever pumped it up and down. "You must be so proud to have raised such a fine young man," she said. She grabbed Dad's hand, too, and shook that. Dad simply stared at her.

"Well, well, I must be off," she said. "I'll be back in two weeks." She raced to the door.

Anthony followed. He was getting used to moving quickly around her. "But wait!" he yelled. "I don't know your name, or where you're going."

She stopped. "Oh, how silly of me, I've forgotten to tell you my name. It's Hilda, my dear. Hilda E. Everring."

"Nice to meet you, Miss Everring," Anthony said.

She bowed. "The same, I'm sure."

She was out the door.

Anthony followed. "But Miss Everring, where are you . . ."

It was too late. She was gone.

5

"Well, Anthony," Mom said later that evening, "it's nice to see you're making a little money—just as long as you keep that . . .that . . .that . . .thing in your room."

"And when you get an idea like this in the future, you've got to ask us first, understand?"

"Yes, Dad." Anthony hadn't told that he was going to give the money to them, and he wasn't going to tell now, either, not

until Miss Everring got home from where-
ever she was and paid him.

Boy, would they be surprised! Mom
could buy lots of tea, with two dollars a
day. Miss Everring was going to be gone for
two weeks! Let's see, that was fourteen
days times two dollars a day. Wow!
Twenty-eight dollars. Maybe that could
help pay for Dad's visits to the chiropractor, just a little.

Anthony knew Dad was worried about
that. Last night, before he went to sleep,
Anthony had heard Dad tell Mom that
maybe he should skip some appointments
because of the cost.

Mom hadn't gotten mad this time.
She'd only said, "Leonard, try not to worry
so much. We'll be okay. We'll make it
somehow."

Anthony pressed his lips together.

Mom had said not to worry. But Anthony was really glad he had a job.

Anthony wanted to find a perfect place for Norman, near the radiator so he'd be warm, but high up so he could see things. The top of his bureau would work.

He took his denim jacket off the bureau and placed his mineral collection neatly on the floor. There, that was a good spot for Norman's home.

Norman was amazing. The fat belly part of him was so black and so shiny, and the tips of his legs had that same lovely velvet as his body. Anthony longed to touch him, to see how he would feel. Speckles jumped onto the top of the bureau to have a look. Norman didn't seem to mind. He just sat on his big rock in the center of the fish tank.

There were three rocks in there, two

flat ones on the bottom and one larger one for Norman to climb. Miss Everring had placed a plastic cactus near the center of the tank, and if Anthony scrunched up his eyes, he could pretend Norman was in the desert.

Anthony took the plastic container and put it down next to Norman's home, but then he picked it up again and left it on the other side of his room on the little table next to his bed. No sense making the crickets stare at Norman all day. Anthony wasn't sure if the crickets knew what was in store for them, but why take any chances?

Anthony didn't like the cricket-feeding part. The thought of it made him feel creepy. Maybe James would do it.

"Mom, can I call James to come down and meet Norman?"

"No, dear, it's getting late. He can meet him tomorrow."

***

"He's amazing," James said. "Let's take him to school and scare all the kids. No, maybe that's not such a great idea. Let's charge kids a quarter to come here to see him. Hey, can I feed him a cricket?"

"She says not to feed him till tomorrow," Anthony said, pulling a list from his pocket. It was the instructions Miss Everring had given him the night before.

1. Change Norman's water every day.
2. Clean his cage once a week—get Norman out by nudging him with a pencil

*into a plastic container. Cover the
container immediately!*

    *3. Don't pick Norman up—he could die
if he were dropped.*

    *4. You can feed him a cricket on
Saturday—he usually eats five or six a
week.*

All of that had seemed normal enough
to Anthony. It was the type of list that
Anthony would have expected from a pet-
sitting client, but the next entries
surprised him.

    *5. Talk to Norman every day—he gets
lonely in his cage and needs some
attention—he likes to be told how
beautiful his hair is.*

    *6. Norman likes a radio on in the late
afternoon.*

*7. Don't be fooled—he's fast. Even
though he'll sit for hours, he can move
like lightning if he wants to, and he won't
come when he's called if he gets away.*

*8. GOOD LUCK, BE BRAVE. You're
doing a noble deed!*

"C'mon, let's feed him a cricket,"
James said.

"We're not supposed to feed him till
tomorrow."

"Yeah, but it says that he won't eat if
he's not hungry—c'mon, we can watch the
cricket jump around."

"That's disgusting."

"You don't want to feed him? You look
a little sick. You look like—"

"James!"

"What?"

"If you stop bugging me, I'll let you

feed Norman a cricket tomorrow."

"Really? Wow, that'd be great. Boy, I've never fed a tarantula before. Can I tell all the kids, can I bring some of 'em over? Can I—"

"If you bring people over, they'll want to feed him, too." Anthony didn't want a lot of kids over. It wasn't just that Dad was always tired and dressed in his pajamas and wasn't friendly and happy like he used to be. Anthony didn't want to scare Norman with a lot of new people. He was starting to believe that Norman was sensitive. And, he wanted to keep Norman to himself.

6

"Gimme the cricket," James said.

Anthony had already lifted the wire mesh off the fish tank and was peering in, studying Norman. The spider was crouched near the big rock, perfectly still. "I got my hands full," he said. "Pick one out yourself." He had brought the plastic container over and set it on the floor. Speckles was examining it.

"You just don't want to do it," James

said. He shooshed Speckles away and selected a cricket. "Oh boy, where should I put it? Maybe I should just drop it in his cage, but he looks like he's not doing anything. He hasn't moved. Is he dead? We haven't seen him move for an hour."

"Just do it and get it over with."

James pulled over a nearby chair and stepped onto it.

And that's when it happened. James bent down and placed the cricket right in front of Norman. But instead of Norman acting interested in his meal, he suddenly sprinted up James's arm.

James jumped off the chair. "Oh, look, yike! Grab him!"

"I can't. Get down!"

"Whaddaya mean?"

"James, lie *down*. Get down on the floor."

"You crazy? He's in my hair."

"Get down! If he jumps off your head, he'll break."

"You're worried about *him*? What about *me*?"

"Stop jumping. Get down!"

James stared at Anthony. He got down on his hands and knees and then slid to hug the floor. Norman sat for a minute and then calmly walked onto his nose.

"Help!"

"Be quiet, you're scaring him!"

"Scaring *him*!"

Norman took a little leap and landed safely on the floor next to Anthony. Pausing only for a moment, he scampered toward the bureau.

Anthony blocked his path with the wire mesh top.

Norman scurried toward the bed.

James put a shoe in his path.

Norman made a dash toward the heating grate next to the door.

"Look out, he's making a run for it!"

"If he gets into that, we've lost him for sure."

And that's when Anthony learned he was good in emergencies. He calmly placed the wire mesh flat on the floor in Norman's path, and Norman scrambled onto it. Anthony quickly picked up the mesh, pushed it into the cage and nudged the back end of Norman until he dashed off to reenter captivity. Anthony placed the wire mesh firmly back on top and weighted it down with his shoe.

"Hey, that was great!" James said. "Where'd you learn to do that?"

Anthony sat down on the floor, limp from the excitement. "I don't know. Miss

Everring's instructions said I could nudge him with a pencil, so I . . ." He picked up Speckles, who was sniffing around the bureau.

"He's fast! He's like a track star, he's like a . . . Hey, maybe we could enter him in some contest."

"James?"

"Yeah?"

"Let's be happy we didn't lose him. Think of what it would've been like telling Miss Everring, not to mention my mom."

James sat down next to him on the floor and petted Speckles, too. "You're right. Next time, I'm just going to drop the cricket in."

"What's going on in here?" It was Dad, standing in the doorway.

"Nothing, Dad."

"I thought I heard some excitement."

It was probably the way Dad said it that made Anthony decide to tell him. Dad sounded a little like his old self, and he was smiling. "Norman escaped, up James's arm!"

"Yeah, and then he was heading for the heating grate and—"

"Wow, and then he would have been gone forever." Dad walked over to the bureau and looked in Norman's cage. "Or even worse, he might've gotten loose in the house and wound up somewhere unannounced . . . like in your mother's cereal bowl!" Dad laughed.

Dad was laughing? Anthony watched him. Even Dad's eyes had a sparkle.

Anthony smiled. He hadn't seen Dad laugh like that since he had gotten hurt.

7

The telephone call for Anthony's
second pet-sitting job came on Monday
afternoon, just as Anthony and James were
getting ready to feed Norman. It was Mr.
Abelson, the neighbor from two houses
down.

"Going to visit my daughter. Got a
chance to stay over a few days," he said.
"The cats are getting on in years, but I
know you'll do a good job taking care

of them. When can you come over to get the key?"

"Now?" Anthony asked.

"Good enough."

"Wow," Anthony said as he placed the phone carefully on the receiver. He turned to James. "I'm gonna be rich. But I'm gonna wait till Miss Everring comes back before I give Mom and Dad the money. Then I can give 'em a pile."

He walked back into his bedroom and handed the cricket container to James. Then he lifted the wire mesh off Norman's cage.

"Here's a nice, juicy, fat one," James said as he grabbed a cricket.

Anthony scrunched up his eyes. "Just do it."

"Hey, I didn't make up this nature stuff," James said.

"Yeah, but you don't have to *enjoy* it."

Placing the cricket a few inches from Norman, James quickly withdrew his hand. He wasn't having Norman using his arm as a getaway ramp a second time.

Anthony covered the cage. Then they watched. And waited. Nothing happened. Norman just sat there.

"Maybe we should put the cricket closer," James said. "Maybe he can't see it. Maybe he—"

"He sure saw the one you put in there on Saturday."

"Yeah, after he almost escaped! Hey, he'll probably eat it if we leave him alone."

James had a point. They could check on Norman and the cricket when they got home from Mr. Abelson's. Anthony grabbed his denim jacket off the bed. As he reached his door, he glanced back, just in case something had happened. But, no, Norman was still ignoring the cricket.

"He'll eat it by the time we get back," Anthony said. But even to himself, he didn't sound sure.

✳✳✳

"Spike and Zeke," Mr. Abelson said as he pointed to the two black-and-white tuxedo cats looking like commas on the couch. He bent down and picked up a third cat—an enormous orange tabby stretched out on the floor. "And this is Puddles. Poor thing," he said. "Arthritic—in her hind legs. She hasn't been the same since she can't jump into her favorite chair anymore."

Mr. Abelson carefully placed Puddles

in the overstuffed rocker in front of the television. She licked his finger, and he rubbed her face. "I'd be mighty obliged if you could put her up here for a few minutes when you're taking care of the cats. You've got to lift her back down, too."

"How much does she weigh?" asked Anthony.

"Sixteen, eighteen, maybe twenty pounds. But she used to be a frolicky little kitten at heart, before her legs went bad."

"How come you named her Puddles?" James asked before Anthony's warning glance could stop him.

Mr. Abelson laughed. "Not the reason you think. Even when she was a kitten, she was pretty big. Looked like a puddle of fur to me wherever she lay down."

Anthony frowned. Now, Norman was a

nice name, a sensible name. Anthony wondered if Norman had eaten his cricket yet.

"Now, about their food," Mr. Abelson said, walking into the kitchen. He motioned for Anthony and James to follow. "Feed them tomorrow afternoon and then twice a day after that. Spike and Zeke get fed near the refrigerator, and Puddles gets her supper under the table."

Anthony nodded.

"You know how to use a cassette recorder?" Mr. Abelson asked.

"Yes," said Anthony.

Mr. Abelson handed him a tape. "Play this while you're feeding them. It's me reading poetry." He opened a cabinet, pulled out a tape recorder, and placed it on the table. Turning to Anthony, he said, "They get lonely when I'm gone."

*** *** ***

Both of them went right to Anthony's
bedroom as soon as they got home.
Norman hadn't moved! The cricket was
jumping around the tarantula's water bowl.

"Maybe he's sick," James said, peering
closely at the spider.

Anthony sank limply onto his bed.

James kept talking. "Yeah, that's it.
He's probably just not hungry. Remember
the cricket I gave him Saturday? That was
a big one, and I bet that—"

"James?"

"Yeah?"

"Let's get the cricket out of there."

"You sure?"

"How would you like to be in a cage,
staring at something that thinks you're
supper?"

James sighed. He reached into the cage and tried to capture the cricket, which kept jumping away. "Tomorrow," he said, when he finally had the cricket safely in his hand, "tomorrow, I'll bet Norman is going to be starved!"

8

"Where's Spike?" Anthony asked,
standing in Mr. Abelson's living room on
Tuesday afternoon. Zeke was staring at
them with circle-perfect eyes from his spot
on the couch, and Puddles was sitting on
Anthony's foot. "We didn't let him out
when we came in, did we?"

"Maybe he's in the bedroom. Maybe he
got locked up in the closet. Maybe he got
out on Mr. Abelson. Maybe—"

"I'll take the bedroom and you check the porch."

Anthony looked in all the obvious places: under the bed and in back of the bureau and even behind Mr. Abelson's huge, cluttered desk. Remembering how Speckles liked to play with his socks, Anthony opened all the dresser drawers to see if Spike might have gotten closed in by mistake. Then he pulled Mr. Abelson's chair over to the closet to check on the top shelf.

"Isn't Mr. Abelson going to get mad at us for going through his stuff?" James asked, standing in the doorway.

"He's going to get a lot madder if we lose his cat," Anthony answered.

"Maybe Spike's back in the living room."

"Why should he just show up?" But

Anthony followed his friend, hoping that James was right. He stopped in the open doorway and stared at the couch. "Oh no! Now *Zeke* is gone!"

James sank into Puddles's chair. The older cat tried to jump into his lap, but her hind legs collapsed and she fell back.

"Me-oww."

"Poor kitty." Anthony sat down next to her on the floor and lifted her onto his lap.

"I think we should stick with tarantu-las," James said.

That was too much! Suddenly, all that Anthony could see was Norman, sitting motionless in his cage all morning, while James put cricket after cricket in front of him. They'd tried five separate times, and even once this afternoon before they'd left. Norman hadn't cared. Norman hadn't seemed to notice. The tarantula *had* spun a web in his cage during the night, but other than that, he wasn't doing anything.

Anthony carefully placed Puddles back on the floor and then stood up. "Let's check the top of the refrigerator," he said. "Some cats like to sleep up there."

When Anthony first walked into the kitchen, he saw something but he couldn't figure out what it was. Then he laughed.

"Hey, why're you stopping? We should check the cabinets and—"

"James?"

"Yeah?"

"Look!" Anthony could only point to two large pots on Mr. Abelson's kitchen table. From the top of one a speck of black was hanging over the edge. It was the tip of a tail!

Anthony ran. Looking inside, he saw a whiskered face peering up at him. Spike!

Zeke was in the other pot, purring softly.

"Pfew!" Anthony said, lifting out Spike. "I'm sure glad to see you guys."

After they fed the cats, Anthony remembered the tape that Mr. Abelson wanted them to play. "Let's bring it into the living room," he told James, "so Puddles can rest in her chair."

The five of them listened, three of them purring, while Mr. Abelson's voice read poems about cats.

"I didn't know there were so many cat poems," James said when the tape was finished.

"Me neither," Anthony answered. "I think Mr. Abelson made up some of them."

✳✳✳

Norman was the same when they got back, huddled at the far edge of the tank, showing no interest in the crickets James placed before him. "What're we gonna do?"

"Try again tomorrow," James said.

"I'll bet he misses Miss Everring. I'll bet that's why he's not eating."

James gave him a long look. "C'mon. He probably doesn't even know she's gone."

"You don't know how tarantulas feel," Anthony said.

"At least Norman's not escaping."

Anthony thought about that scary time. But then something about the memory of Norman sprinting up James's arm made him keep on thinking. Something about Norman dashing up and out, where he wanted to go . . . and

Puddles not being able to jump . . .

"James—you're brilliant!"

"I am? What'd I do?"

"C'mon. Dad's got the tools in the van, and I'm sure there's a few pieces of scrap wood in there."

"Anthony, what're you talking about?"

"A ramp. We're gonna build a ramp. For Puddles. So she can walk up into her chair."

At least it was something. At least it was one thing Anthony could do to make some animal happy.

Anthony turned away from Norman's cage. But he couldn't stop himself from looking back as he left his bedroom.

9

They had to wait for half an hour before Dad woke up. He was still sleeping every afternoon.

"Hey, Dad, can I have the key to the van?" Anthony asked. "And can I use some scrap wood? I'm building something," he added.

Before, Dad would have asked him what he was working on. Before, Dad would have come down and gotten the tools out and asked him if he needed help. Before, Dad liked teaching Anthony how to make things with wood.

But today, Dad just went back silently into his bedroom and got the key for the work van. He handed it to Anthony, then sat down at the kitchen table and stared out the window.

"Want a snack, Leonard?" Mom asked, coming into the kitchen. "Or a cup of coffee?"

"It's taking so long," Dad said. "I'm still so sick. And so *weak*. I'll never get back to work."

Mom kissed Dad's forehead. "Try not to worry," she said. She sat down next to him. "It's normal to feel discouraged."

Anthony was tired of feeling discouraged. He wanted to *do* something. He'd worked with Dad a little last summer, and he knew enough about carpentry to make a good ramp.

Anthony and James went back over to Mr. Abelson's and took measurements of the chair. Then, in the van, they cut the long, flat board and the two triangle pieces and hammered them together.

"Look at that," Anthony said, as he tossed a scrap of wood into a box in the corner. He reached over and pulled a long, skinny piece of brown carpet from under the box. "This is perfect. It's just about the right size."

"Whaddaya want it for?" James asked.

"It'll cover the top of the ramp, so Puddles's claws will have something to grab onto as she walks up."

"Shouldn't you ask your Dad about using the carpet?" James asked.

Anthony shrugged. He probably should.

He would have, before. But today, Dad seemed so quiet, so unhappy.

Anthony hammered the last nail. "C'mon, James, let's take this over," he said. "Let's see if Puddles likes it."

✳✳✳

They placed the ramp in front of the chair, and Puddles sniffed it from the bottom to as far up as she could reach.

"Mee-ow!"

Twitching her tail and moving to face the ramp, Puddles set one paw onto the walkway and then a second. She yowled and then marched on all fours up the runway. She settled into her chair, purring loudly.

"All right!" Anthony said.

"Gimme five!" said James.

As they sat there listening to Puddles purring, Anthony forgot, for a few minutes at least, all about Norman.

But when he got home, there was a postcard waiting for him on the kitchen table.

Dear Anthony,
Having a wonderful time! It feels so good to know that Norman is in such capable hands! Tell him I miss him!
Sincerely,
Miss Hilda E. Everring

P.S. I've adopted some new friends that I can't wait to have you meet!

The postcard showed a mother and baby kangaroo in the Australian outback. Did that mean Miss Everring was in

Australia? And who . . . or what were her new friends?

Anthony held the postcard up to Norman's cage. He showed Norman the picture side and then Miss Everring's writing. "Look, Norman," he said. "She's thinking about you. She'll be home soon. Honest." But Norman didn't move. He didn't seem interested in anything. He was acting just like Dad.

10

It had already been one of the worst
days of Anthony's life. At breakfast, when
Mom had given Anthony his bowl of
oatmeal, he had gotten the jar of walnuts
out of the cupboard.

"Those cost money, you know!" Dad
had said in an angry voice.

"Leonard," Mom said, "this is ridicu-
lous! Anthony can have walnuts if he
likes. We're not so poor."

"We're going to be that poor if I can't work. What good's a carpenter with a bad back?" Dad slammed his cup of coffee onto the table so hard that the coffee splattered. Then he left the kitchen. Anthony heard the bedroom door bang shut.

"It's okay, honey," Mom said. "He's just worried. He's been hurting a long time now, and it's wearing on him."

But Anthony thought that Dad's back was getting better. Dad was walking more naturally now, and he was even sleeping through the night, not waking up with his back hurting anymore.

Wasn't Dad getting better? Were they going to be so poor that Anthony could never again have walnuts on his oatmeal?

When Anthony got to school that morning, he failed his math test. He couldn't concentrate. Besides, he was hungry. He hadn't been able to finish his oatmeal after Dad had yelled at him.

It was spaghetti day, but Anthony spent the dollar Mom had given him because he was really starved. He felt feelings inside that he didn't understand, and he hoped the spaghetti might take them away.

It didn't. The spaghetti only made him feel a little sick.

✳✳✳

Now the long day at school was finally over, and Anthony and James were in Anthony's bedroom watching Norman. Again they examined the beautiful web that Norman had spun in his home, the long web that reached from one end of the fish tank to the other.

But Norman was sick, or might be.

Anthony had only taken care of him for a week, and he might be sick!

Anthony stared at the spider. Norman was less shiny somehow, a less bright black. And there were little drops of liquid on his legs! "Hey, James," he said. "Look at this, look at his legs. Is that his blood?"

"But it's not red."

"Maybe tarantulas have clear blood."

James bent closer to Norman's cage. "Yeah, and look how he's just sitting there, not doing anything."

"He's done that before."

"But not in the corner like that, see? And he's on his side!"

James was right. Norman was crouching in the corner behind his web, legs curled under him. Well, that proved it; all the signs were there. Norman still wasn't eating. His belly *was* duller, and he was bleeding! And now this crouching in the corner.

Norman *was* sick! Miss Everring was going to come home and find out that Anthony had let Norman get sick.

Anthony stood up and walked over to his window. He looked down at the collie next door, tied up and barking. It wasn't fair. Norman never barked. He was quiet and clean, and the other day when Anthony had cleaned his cage, he had actually come close, as though he was saying hello.

It wasn't fair. Why did Norman have to get sick? Tears came into Anthony's eyes.

But wait, he'd thought of something. Anthony took off his glasses and rubbed his eyes. He knew what he had to do.

"C'mon, James," he said. "Leave him alone. Let's go tell Dad."

11

"You want to take Norman to the *vet?*"
Dad was yelling—for the second time that
day!

Anthony should have remembered. Dad
was different now. He should have waited
for Mom. Mom was still the same, almost
still the same, even though she was
working all the time.

"It's a spider, it's a stupid spider, and
we don't have the money!"

How could Dad say that? How could Dad call Norman a stupid spider? He was a wonderful spider, and he was Anthony's responsibility.

But Dad was still yelling. "Just because you want to make some money to buy a bike or a Walkman or something it's going to cost us money?"

Something burst in Anthony, some of the feelings that the spaghetti hadn't been able to get rid of. "I'm supposed to take care of him!" He was yelling, actually yelling at Dad! "All you care about is money! You don't even care about Norman. You don't even care about me!" He started to run out of the kitchen, but James was standing there.

Oh, great! James was seeing him crying. James had seen him yell at Dad.

But James was just standing there

quietly, and then he said something that was none of his business. In a soft voice, so low that Anthony almost couldn't hear him, he said, "But he's giving the money to you."

Dad stared at him. "What did you say?"

Anthony didn't have time to give James a warning look, and this time James spoke in a loud, clear voice. "He's not saving the money for himself. He's going to give the money to you."

Dad sat down. "You're saving the money for Mom and me? That's why you're doing this pet-sitting thing?"

Anthony wouldn't answer. He was crying freely now. James had told. James had never told before.

Then Dad did something that made Anthony forget about James. Dad put his head down on the table and started to cry.

Anthony almost ran to him. He wanted to, but he was scared. Dad was different now, so different. What if he started yelling again?

James turned and opened the kitchen door and walked down the back stairs. Anthony was glad.

Dad was still crying. Anthony walked slowly back to his bedroom. Standing in his doorway, he looked in at his room, the room that he knew so thoroughly: his mineral collection lining the window sill, his ocean book Grandma had sent from New Jersey for Christmas, the space shuttle he'd made out of Legos in second grade. It was so familiar, so comforting, so good to at least have his room stay the same.

Anthony looked toward his bureau and saw Norman huddled in the corner. He went closer. Norman had his legs curled under him. He hadn't moved at all.

Anthony turned and pulled his denim jacket off the peg behind his door. He knew what he had to do. Grabbing the quilt Mom had made, he put it over Norman's tank and lifted the tank into his arms.

If Dad wouldn't help, that was too bad, but it was okay. Anthony would just have to help Norman all by himself.

He'd had to wait for an hour in Dr. Reese's reception area. He sat there, holding the fish tank on his lap, trying to keep Norman warm. With Norman being sick, that was especially important, he thought.

The waiting room was crowded. On Anthony's left was a man holding a squirming kitten. On his right sat a boy, not much older than himself, with a beige

Lab on a leash. The dog was lying on the floor, head on paws. His eyes were pink, and every few minutes he groaned.

"What's the matter with him?" Anthony asked.

"Oh, he's eating things again," the boy said, almost in a whisper. "He got my mother's old wig this time."

Bending down to look more closely at the dog, Anthony asked, "He eats things?"

"Yeah, candies—wrapped candies— pillows, trash, you name it."

"Wow." Boy, Norman never did anything like that! Miss Everring was right, tarantulas were a lot smarter than dogs.

The Lab groaned again.

"What's his name?" Anthony asked.

"Clyde."

"Will he be okay?"

"I think so. He's been okay all the other times, but my mother sure is mad about her wig. She says it had sentimental value."

∗∗∗

Dr. Reese smiled as he called them into the examining room. "Hi, Anthony," he said. "How's Speckles?"

"Fine."

"Do your dad and mom know you're here?"

Anthony pushed his glasses back up on his nose. "Well . . . Dr. Reese?"

"Yes, Anthony."

"Can I pay you later, like when I get paid? See, I'm pet-sitting him."

"Hm. . . I see. Let's not talk about that now. Let's look at this fine creature you have here." He lifted the quilt off the cage and peered in. Then he opened a drawer and took out a huge magnifying glass. He studied Norman. "Amazing," he said.

"Is he going to die?" Anthony asked. Somehow, the tears were threatening to come back.

"Now, tell me the symptoms."

"He hasn't been eating, and he's just been sitting there in that funny position."

"And his belly's turned duller, hasn't it?"

Anthony nodded.

"Little spots of liquid on his legs?"

Oh, it must be something really bad if Dr. Reese knew that already! Anthony wiped his face with the back of his hand. "Yes," he answered.

"Well, young man," Dr. Reese said, smiling, "you have a fine young tarantula

here who is molting."

"Molting?" Did that mean he was going to die?

"Molting, changing skin. Tarantulas do that just like snakes do, once or twice a year. C'mere, look, he's already started." Dr. Reese handed Anthony the magnifying glass and motioned for him to bend down.

Looking in, looking closely, Anthony could see an extra piece of skin on the end of Norman's leg. Oh, no, that was his old skin! "Is he going to be okay?"

"Better than that. In just a few hours, you are going to have a tarantula with a fine new skin. But you must not touch him for a few days. He'll be sensitive for a while."

It was wonderful news, but Anthony felt like crying even more! Norman was going to be okay! And Anthony was going to be able to watch him coming out of his skin.

"And," Dr. Reese went on, "by tomorrow or the next day at the latest, he'll probably be ravenous, so you might want to feed him extra." He reached over and handed Anthony a tissue. "And you'd better take care of that cold," he said.

"Dr. Reese?" Anthony blew his nose.

"Yeah?"

"How much do I owe you?"

"Oh, pay me a dollar when you can. Consultations on molting tarantulas are a dollar."

13

Dad didn't seem surprised when
Anthony walked in the door holding
Norman. Dad was sitting at the table
drinking a cup of coffee. He'd combed his
hair and gotten dressed, put on tan pants
and his good flannel shirt. "How is
Norman?" he asked. He didn't seem mad.

"He's okay." Anthony stood there,
wishing he could get into his room
without going past Dad.

"Sit down, Anthony." Dad pointed to the chair next to him. "And put Norman on the counter over there, away from the window—there's a draft."

Those five steps over to the counter and back seemed to take forever.

"What's the matter with him?" Dad sounded really interested.

"He's molting."

Dad laughed. "They molt? They shed their skins, like snakes?"

"Yeah." Anthony was still looking down at his feet. He shouldn't have disobeyed Dad. He didn't have to take Norman to Dr. Reese after all. Norman was okay—he was just molting.

Dad laughed again. "Well, I'm still glad you took him. This way, we won't have to worry."

"I'm gonna pay for it myself."

"It's okay, you did the right thing. I was wrong."

What? Dad was apologizing?

"Listen—I've been feeling sorry for myself. I've been worrying about how long it's taking me to recover, and if I'm ever going to be well enough to work." He reached over and touched Anthony lightly on his cheek. "I haven't even been grateful that I *am* getting better. But you know what made the difference?"

"What?"

"I helped raise a fine son. I can't be all that much of a failure. And maybe I should use some of that gumption my son has. You started a business, all on your own. If it turns out I can't build porches anymore, I'll figure out something else."

"You're not mad at me for taking Norman to the vet?"

"No, you had to. I'm proud of you."

Anthony felt so tired. But a smile was starting to grow deep within him. "You want to see Norman molt?" he asked.

"Sure."

Anthony brought Norman's tank over to the table. Norman had withdrawn from the skin of two legs already, just on the trip home from Dr. Reese's.

Anthony pulled his chair up next to Dad so they could both see clearly. Speckles tried to join them on the third chair, but Anthony told her no, thinking that Norman probably wouldn't want a cat staring at him while he was working so hard. Dad and Anthony sat there, not talking, just watching Norman.

The spider was still in the corner, but less crouched over now. He stopped and rested for a few minutes, but then

withdrew from another leg.

"Fascinating," Dad said. "I hope I can get rid of my old skin that easily."

He sounded like Dad, the old Dad. Anthony turned sideways and hugged him. Dad held him close and kissed the top of his head.

***

When Mom got home from work, she found them at the table, staring at Norman. "You're dressed," she said to Dad. She didn't seem to notice Norman.

Dad got up and kissed her. She sat down and looked at the cage, and then looked at Dad and Anthony.

"Something's different," she said.

"You got it," Dad said. "And to celebrate, why don't we go out for ice cream after supper."

Ice cream? On a weeknight? Boy, things were different—*good* different this time.

"Can I ask James to come, too?" Anthony asked.

"Sure, give him a call."

Anthony brought Norman back into his bedroom. Maybe Norman would like to be in a familiar place while he was molting. Laying the tank gently down on the bureau, Anthony noticed the postcard from Miss Everring. Boy, she'd sure be surprised to find out that Norman had molted! And who *were* those new friends she was bringing from Australia?

Anthony took a step back, then touched his fingers to his forehead in a salute. "Thanks, Norman," he said. "Thanks for being okay."

14

Anthony had Norman's old skin ready for Miss Everring the following Thursday. Dad helped him make a special box for it out of thin strips of wood, and Anthony placed it next to the tank on the bureau. Norman ignored it.

Dr. Reese had been right. After he'd finished molting, Norman had been quiet for two days. But since then he'd been pouncing on every single cricket that had been put into his cage.

Now Anthony and James were sitting at the kitchen table playing Connect Four. "When's she coming back?" James asked.

There was an answering knock on the door.

"Well, well, my fine young friends," Miss Everring said, hurrying into the kitchen. She was wearing her long blue coat and, this time, had orange ribbons in her flyaway hair. "I've had the most fabulous time, most fabulous," she said. "But I can't wait to see my Norman. It's amazing how that little creature can spin his web into your heart."

Anthony laughed as he went to get Norman. "Here he is," he said proudly, as he returned to the kitchen with the spider.

"Oh my, Norman! You look so wonderful!"

Was Miss Everring going to be able to see that Norman had molted? Anthony wanted to tell her himself, with his present.

Setting the fish tank onto the table, Anthony went back to get his surprise. But as he returned to the kitchen, the doorbell rang. Who could it be? Mom had gone with Dad to the chiropractor just half an hour ago.

"Who is it?" he asked.

"Mr. Abelson."

James opened the door. Mr. Abelson took off his hat and bowed to Miss Everring. Then he handed Anthony a package, all wrapped up with brightly colored paper. "A present," he said. "For building that wonderful ramp for Puddles. She's like her old self. Walks up and down, up and down. Loves it. And here's ten dollars for all your trouble."

Wow—*ten dollars*! Anthony thanked Mr. Abelson. Then he opened the package and discovered a beautiful painting of Puddles, sleeping happily in her chair. "Oh," he said. "It's wonderful!"

"Painted it myself," Mr. Abelson said.

Miss Everring moved closer. "Oh, you're an artist!"

"Poet, too," Mr. Abelson said. "And what do you do, may I ask?"

"I am a biologist," Miss Everring answered.

"Fascinating."

Anthony remembered his gift for Miss Everring. "Something terrific happened," he said. He paused so that he could hold the box a moment longer. Then, sighing, he handed it over.

Opening the box, Miss Everring

jumped. "Oh, he molted. He *molted!* I'm so glad you had a chance to see him do that. And you must have taken such good care of him; he looks so beautiful!" Miss Everring took Norman's old skin out of the box and held it in the palm of her hand.

"You didn't get to see Norman molt, so I thought you'd like to have this," Anthony said.

"Oh, most thoughtful. Most thoughtful, my boy. I have saved and treasured every one of his five old skins. And it's such a lovely box. But . . ." She peered at Norman for a moment. Placing the skin carefully in the box, she gave it back to Anthony. "But this belongs to you. You were with him when he molted."

Anthony couldn't believe his luck. He held the box closely.

"And, here is your remittance."

Remittance? But Anthony understood when Miss Everring handed him the money.

Twenty-eight dollars—plus the ten dollars from Mr. Abelson—he was rich! Mom and Dad could buy a *lot* with thirty-eight dollars!

"Beautiful creature," Mr. Abelson said, bending down to examine Norman. "Always wanted to have a tarantula, but didn't want him scared by the cats."

"A most thoughtful approach," Miss Everring said. "What did you say your name was?"

"Mr. Henry Abelson, at your service." He bowed a second time.

"Hilda Everring," she said, grabbing his hand and shaking it firmly. "Well, well, I must be off. Lots to do, lots to take care of." Miss Everring picked up Norman's tank and headed for the door.

Mr. Abelson followed, and Anthony heard him ask as they were walking down the stairs, "Do you happen to like poetry?"

"Like it, I love it! You don't happen to know any poems about tarantulas . . . ?"

"But Miss Everring," Anthony called, as he raced after them. "Who are the friends that you brought home from Australia?"

Miss Everring stopped. "Oh, did I forget to tell you? My dear, they're wonderful friends, and I can't wait to have you meet them. When you come visit Norman, of course. It's going to be simply marvelous to bring them along on my visits to schools, when I show Norman to the children. Ta-ta!"

"But Miss Everring, who *are* your friends?"

"My new friends, my dear, are Australian myrmecia."

"But Miss Everring . . ." Anthony watched Mr. Abelson and Miss Everring disappear past the second-floor landing. He turned back to James, who was still standing in the kitchen doorway.

"C'mon, James," he said. "Grab our coats. Let's go over to the library and find out what myr . . . what Australian myrmecia are."

CYNTHIA STOWE lives in the hills of western Massachusetts with her husband and two cats. Among her many animal friends have been Ironing Board Kitty; Prince; Meow-Meow and her kittens; Fang; Paws; Freewheel; Ralphie Matt; Silvester; Speckles McGraw; and Boticelli. She has published two other novels for children.

CAT BOWMAN SMITH has illustrated many children's books, including *Matthew the Cowboy* and *Peter's Trucks*, for Albert Whitman and Company. When she is not painting pictures of New York City, where she resides, Cat likes to sail, rollerblade, and visit with her parakeets, Casper and Miniblue.

August. 1995

j
Stowe, Cynthia

Not-so-normal Norman.